For Katy Glennon. Much love. C.M. xxx

First published in Great Britain in 2014
by Boxer Books Limited.

www.boxerbooks.com

Boxer® is a registered trademark of Boxer Books Limited.

Text and illustrations copyright © 2014 Cathy MacLennan

The right of Cathy MacLennan to be identified as the author and
illustrator of this work has been asserted by her
in accordance with the Copyright, Designs and Patents Act, 1988.

A CIP catalogue record for this book available from the British Library upon request.

The illustrations were prepared using acrylic paints on Boston board.
The text is set in Family Dog.

ISBN 978-1-907152-26-9

1 3 5 7 9 10 8 6 4 2

Printed in China.

All of our papers are sourced from managed forests and renewable resources.

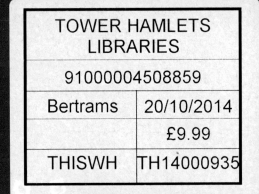

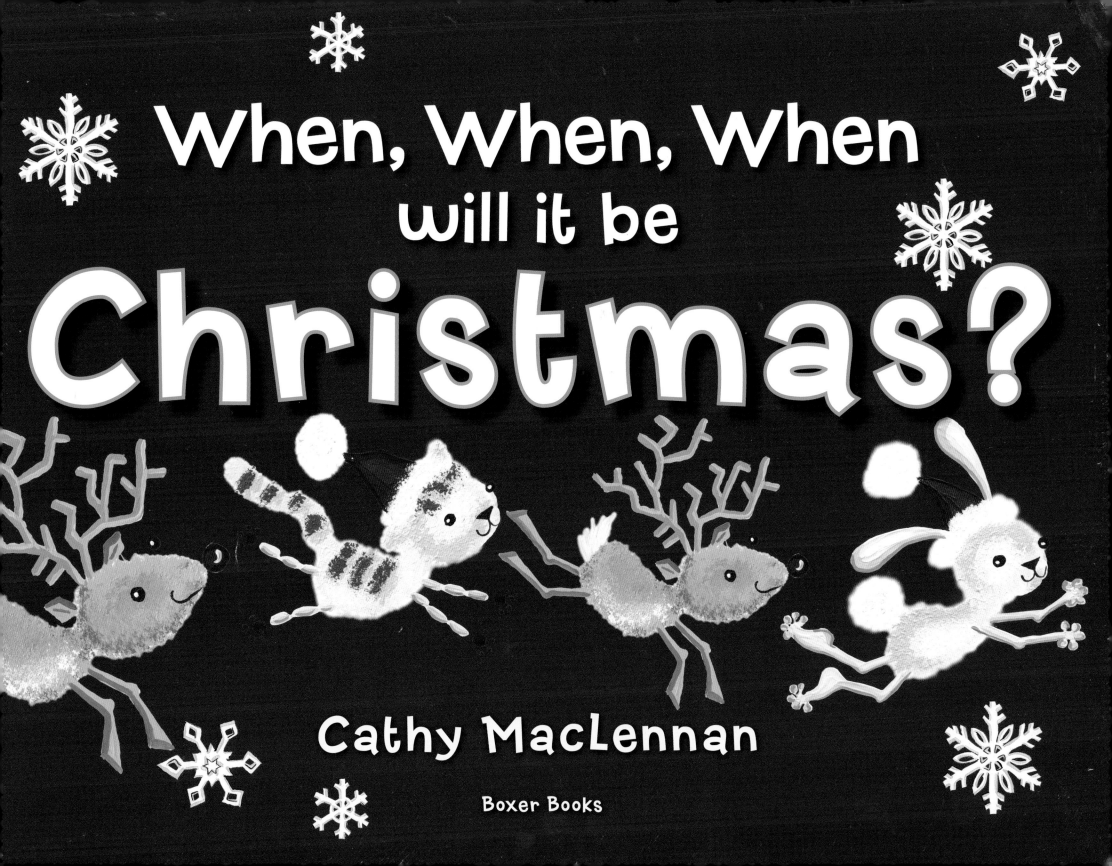

When, When, When will it be Christmas?

Cathy MacLennan

Boxer Books

Red, red birdies with
red, red berries.
Great big bows of red,
red ribbon.
But when will it be Christmas?
Soon, soon, soon.

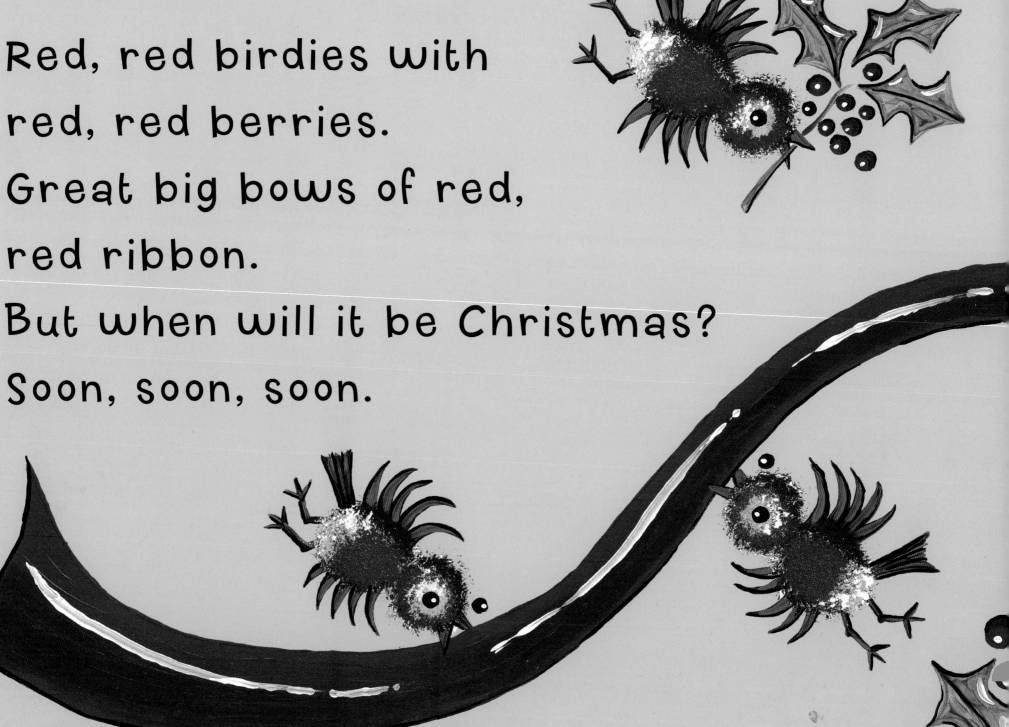

White, white mice
and snipped white snowflakes.
Snip, dance, snip, dance, snip.

Snowy white mice
and white, white icing,
A snow-covered, white-iced
Christmas cake.

But when, when, when will it be Christmas? Soon, soon, soon.

Kittens have chosen a green, green tree,
A beautiful, green, green Christmas tree.

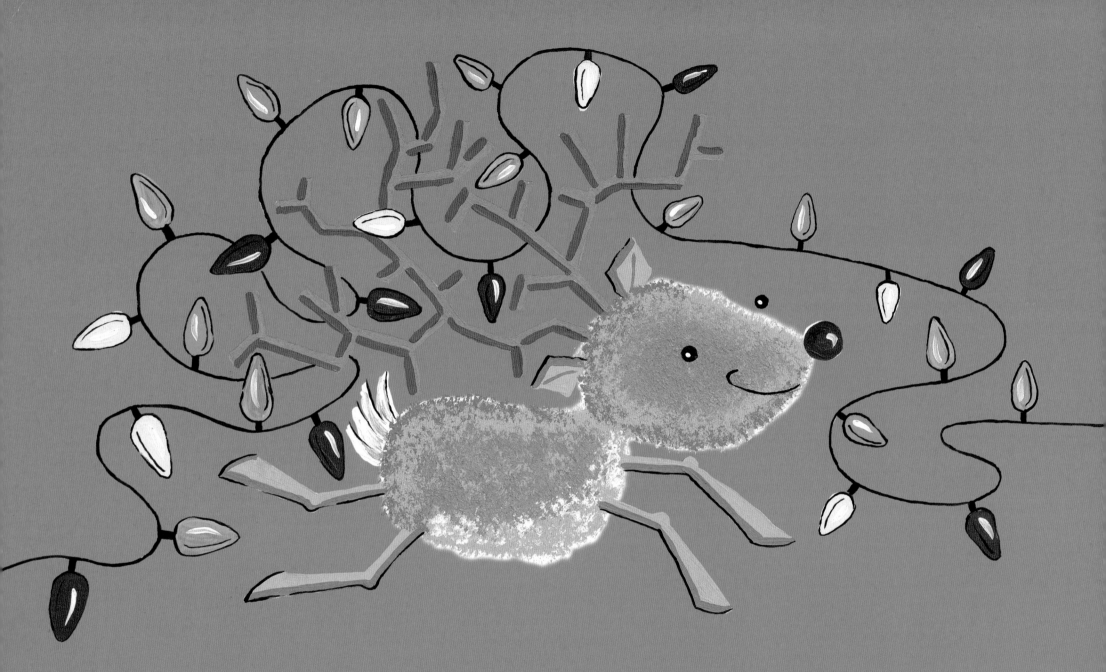

Red-nosed reindeer are hanging lights,
Long, long lines of light-up lights.

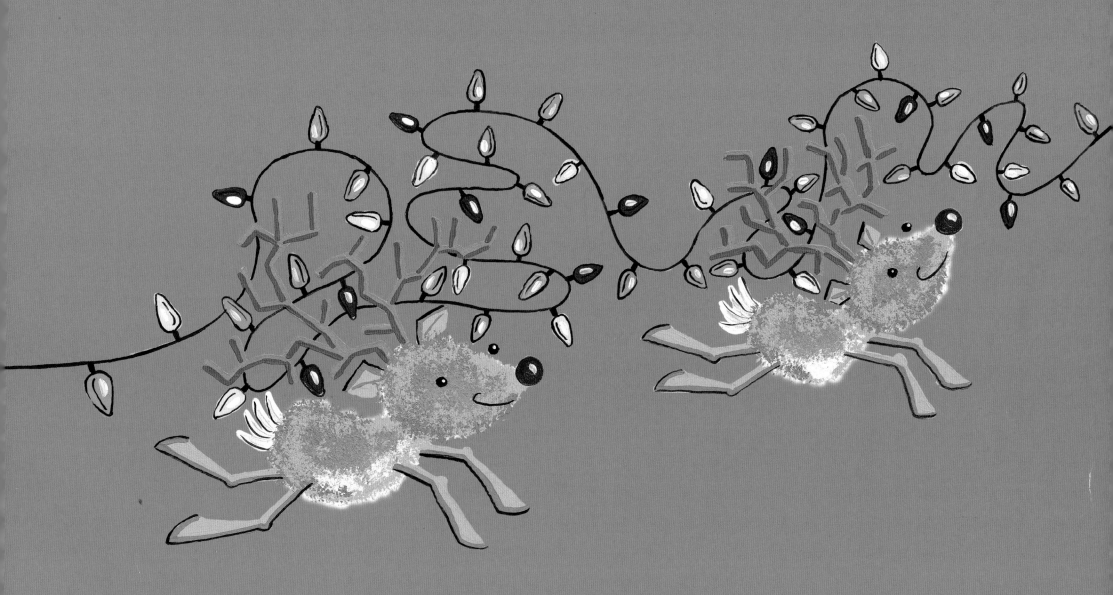

But when, when, when will it be
Christmas? Soon, soon, soon.

Pretty paper, bows and tape,
Rabbits are wrapping, wrapping, wrapping,

Presents, presents . . .

Presents of EVERY size and shape!

But when, oh when, will it be Christmas?
Soon, soon, soon.

Christmas stories and Christmas songs!
Costumes! Scenes! And lights!

A roll of the drum,
And onto the stage . . . they COME!

What a SPECTACULAR Christmas Show!

And the star of the show is . . .

the **STAR!**

Twinkle, twinkle,

TA-DAAAAAH!

But when, oh when, oh when

will it be Christmas?

Soon, soon,

Very, very soon.

Just one more sleep,
It's magical Christmas Eve!

Stockings hung by little beds,
Eyes shut tight,

Kiss-kiss. Night-night.

Then . . .
Twinkle,
twinkle,
Jingle,
jingle.

Wake up birdies!
Wake up rabbits and reindeer.
Wake up kittens!
And snowy, white mice.

Wake up everyone!

It's Christmas!
It's Christmas!!
It's Christmaaaaas!!!

We've waited and waited and waited.
And . . .
It's the BEST Christmas EVER!

Happy, happy
Christmas!